Sir Galahad
and the
Holy Grail

by Karen Wallace and Neil Chapman

W
FRANKLIN WATTS

First published in 2009 by
Franklin Watts
338 Euston Road
London
NW1 3BH

Franklin Watts Australia
Level 17/207 Kent Street
Sydney
NSW 2000

Text © Karen Wallace 2009
Illustrations © Neil Chapman 2009

A CIP catalogue record for this book is available
from the British Library.

ISBN 978 0 7496 8558 4 (hbk)
ISBN 978 0 7496 8570 6 (pbk)

Series Editor: Jackie Hamley
Series Advisor: Dr Barrie Wade
Series Designer: Peter Scoulding

Printed in China

Franklin Watts is a division of
Hachette Children's Books,
an Hachette UK company
www.hachette.co.uk

Sir Lancelot's son, Galahad,
was just a boy when his father
made him a knight.

At exactly the same time, King
Arthur saw Galahad's name
appear on the Round Table.

4

And Sir Kay found a jewelled
sword in a huge stone.
No one could pull it free.

Soon after, an old man walked into Camelot with Sir Galahad. "This knight has a great quest ahead," he said. "He will see the Holy Grail."

The other knights gasped. None of them had ever seen the Holy Grail, but they knew it was the precious cup that Jesus drank from.

When Sir Galahad saw the
jewelled sword, he pulled it free.
Then he joined the other knights
of the Round Table.

Sir Galahad was brave and pure. With his sword, he won many tournaments at Camelot.

One evening the Holy Grail appeared, but only Sir Galahad could see it. "My quest has begun," he cried. "I will find the Holy Grail!"

Sir Perceval, Sir Bors and many other knights also vowed to find it, but Sir Galahad set out alone.

At the start of his journey, Sir Galahad saw a shield in a chapel. "This shield will only protect those who are pure," warned a monk. As he spoke, a prince grabbed the shield and rode off with it.

Immediately, a White Knight knocked the prince off his horse. "This shield belongs to Sir Galahad," he said. "Take it to him!"

The prince gave Sir Galahad the shield. Then Sir Galahad heard a voice say, "Go to the Castle of Maidens and rescue them."

The Castle of Maidens was on the
other side of a huge mountain.
Sir Galahad rode for many days
to reach it.

Seven evil knights attacked
Sir Galahad at the castle gates.
But he fought back with his
sword and shield.

He killed the first knight and the
others ran away. Then he opened
the gates and freed the prisoners.

As a reward for his help, a maiden led Sir Galahad to a magical ship. "To succeed in your quest, you must travel by sea," she told him. "Then find Castle Corbenic. King Pelles looks after the Grail, but he is badly hurt."

Sir Perceval and Sir Bors were already on the ship. The three knights sailed until they reached a strange forest of dead trees.

For many days, the knights rode through the enormous forest.

It was cold and frightening, but at last they found Castle Corbenic.

As King Pelles greeted them, a
procession of four angels suddenly
appeared. One carried a bleeding
spear, another a silver dish and
another a great candlestick. The
last one carried the Holy Grail.

Sir Galahad led the amazing procession up to the castle chapel.

With blood from the bleeding spear, Sir Galahad healed King Pelles' leg and made him well again.

Then Sir Galahad knelt down
in front of the Holy Grail,
and a golden light shone all
around him. At last his great
quest was over!

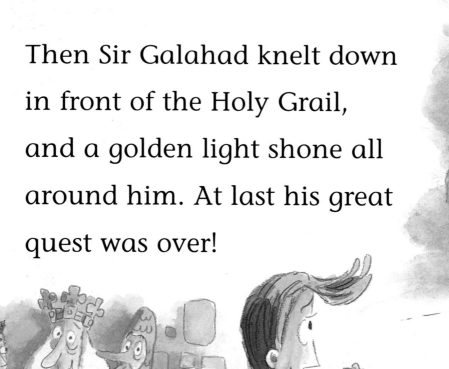

Puzzle 1

Put these pictures in the correct order.
Which event do you think is most important?
Now try writing the story in your own words!

Puzzle 2

1. This belongs to Sir Galahad!

2. I've waited a long time for you knights.

3. I must set the maidens free.

4. I have not walked for many years.

5. I protect this shield. You must be pure to wear it.

6. I shall not rest until I see the Holy Grail.

Choose the correct speech bubbles for the characters above. Can you think of any others? Turn over to find the answers.

Answers

Puzzle 1

The correct order is: 1a, 2f, 3e, 4c, 5b, 6d

Puzzle 2

Sir Galahad: 3, 6

The White Knight: 1, 5

King Pelles: 2, 4

Look out for more Hopscotch Adventures:

TALES OF KING ARTHUR

1. The Sword in the Stone
ISBN 978 0 7496 6694 1

2. Arthur the King
ISBN 978 0 7496 6695 8

3. The Round Table
ISBN 978 0 7496 6697 2

4. Sir Lancelot and the Ice Castle
ISBN 978 0 7496 6698 9

5. Sir Gawain and the Green Knight
ISBN 978 0 7496 8557 7*
ISBN 978 0 7496 8569 0

6. Sir Galahad and the Holy Grail
ISBN 978 0 7496 8558 4*
ISBN 978 0 7496 8570 6

TALES OF ROBIN HOOD

Robin and the Knight
ISBN 978 0 7496 6699 6

Robin and the Monk
ISBN 978 0 7496 6700 9

Robin and the Silver Arrow
ISBN 978 0 7496 6703 0

Robin and the Friar
ISBN 978 0 7496 6702 3

Robin and the Butcher
ISBN 978 0 7496 8555 3*
ISBN 978 0 7496 8568 3

Robin and Maid Marian
ISBN 978 0 7496 8556 0*
ISBN 978 0 7496 8567 6

TALES OF SINBAD THE SAILOR

Sinbad and the Ogre
ISBN 978 0 7496 8559 1*
ISBN 978 0 7496 8571 3

Sinbad and the Whale
ISBN 978 0 7496 8553 9*
ISBN 978 0 7496 8565 2

Sinbad and the Diamond Valley
ISBN 978 0 7496 8554 6*
ISBN 978 0 7496 8566 9

Sinbad and the Monkeys
ISBN 978 0 7496 8560 7*
ISBN 978 0 7496 8572 0

For more *Hopscotch Adventures* and other *Hopscotch* stories, visit:
www.franklinwatts.co.uk

* hardback